You're a Big Brother

Written and illustrated by
Marianne Richmond

sourcebooks
jabberwocky

Copyright © 2017 by Marianne Richmond
Cover and internal design © 2017 by Sourcebooks, Inc.
Cover design by Brittany Vibbert / Sourcebooks, Inc.
Cover images/illustrations © Marianne Richmond

The characters and events portrayed in this book are fictitious and are used fictitiously. Any similarity to real persons, living or dead, is purely coincidental and not intended by the author.

Published by Sourcebooks Jabberwocky, an imprint of Sourcebooks, Inc.
P.O. Box 4410, Naperville, Illinois 60567-4410
(630) 961-3900
Fax: (630) 961-2168
www.sourcebooks.com

Library of Congress Cataloging-in-Publication data is on file with the publisher.

Source of Production: Worzalla, Stevens Point, WI
Date of Production: January 2017
Run Number: 5008366

Printed and bound in the United States of America.
WOZ 10 9 8 7 6 5 4 3 2 1

Dedicated to
the joy of family.

Our baby is coming,
a wee little one.

You're a big brother.
How exciting and fun!

A baby brings changes,
expected and new,
but one thing that *won't* change
is our love for *you.*

At first our new baby
is too little to play,
eating and sleeping
for most of the day.

You did the same things
as a new baby, too.
Now you're our big boy
with lots you can do!

You're a wonderful helper,
and new-diaper bringer,

Toe tickler, nose kisser, and lullaby singer.

You're a peekaboo player
and toy-rattle shaker.

Bubble blower,
hand holder,

and
silly-face
maker.

You're all this and more
that big brothers do.
Then one day—surprise!
A big smile for YOU!

You've made a best friend
and a pal for the park.

You're a
fort maker,

cake baker,

and storyteller
at dark.

Yes, our days will be busy
with baby, it's true,
but we'll always find time
for just me and you.

Our family is growing
in a sweet little way.
You're a **Big Brother!**
Congrats and hooray!

MARIANNE RICHMOND

is the bestselling author of *If I Could Keep You Little*.
She has touched the lives of millions by creating
emotional and thoughtful stories that children
of any age will appreciate now and forever.